holiday time
and no more school.

Drop-it-all Dragon

written by Martin Holland

illustrated by Viktorija Vaitiekute

Fire Breath cave
was quiet and cool,

Mum said "Dragons, before you go, there is something

that you need to know."

"Drop-it-all Dragon
is coming to stay,
his Mum and Dad
are going away.
Lock your toys up,
hide your stuff.
Things might get
a little rough!"

Drag-it-out Dragon thought,
terrible news,
and raced outside,
no time to lose.
He scratched his head
and flapped his wings,
where could he hide
his favourite things?

He still recalled
that dreadful day,
his youngest cousin
came to stay.

The broken bike
and busted toys,
the smell of smoke,
the deafening noise.

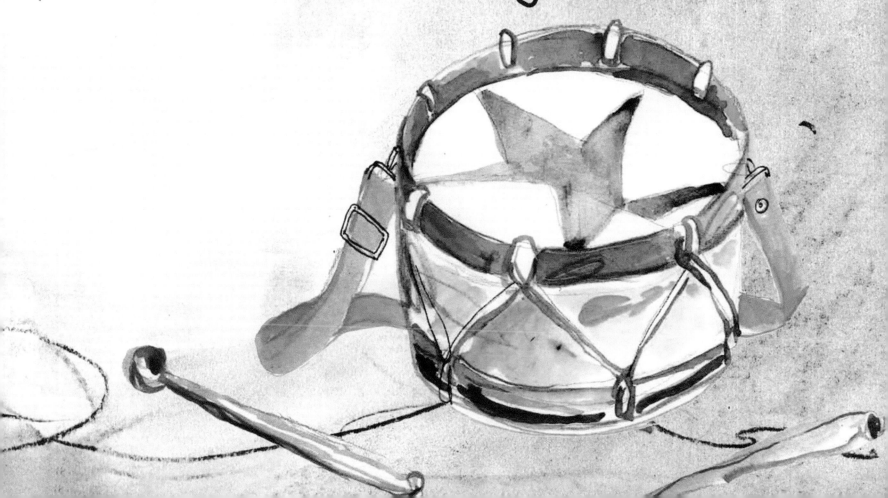

"Come on sis, let's make a plan,
and make things safe
the best we can."

His little sister shook her head,
"I think I'll spend the day in bed!"

Too late,
above them from a cloud,
emerged a dragon,
big and loud.
"Hello cousins,
lovely day,
what fun we're going
to have today."

Crash,
a scooter hit the floor.

Smash,

the ball

went through the door.

The dragon gave
a nervous laugh,
as two more board games
broke in half.

The family yelled out,
with a frown,
"Drop-it-all Dragon
please
put that
down!"

The clumsy dragon
tried his best,

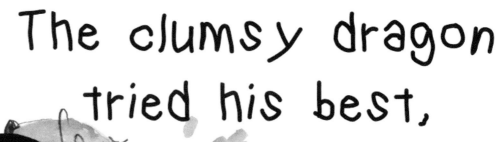

he didn't mean
to be a pest.

But everything he touched

he dropped,

He wished
his problem
could be stopped.

"What's this?
A wizard's cloak and hat,
they have to let me play
with that.
Surely nothing can go wrong?
The peace and calm
did not last long.

The dragon's hands
began to shake,
"Uh oh,
something is going to break."
Both wand and cauldron
hit the ground,
the valley echoed
with the sound.

The family yelled out,
    with a frown,
    "Drop-it-all Dragon
please put
    that
    down!"

They went inside to play a game,
but everything turned out
the same.

Whack,
the cars will need some glue.

Crack,

the drumsticks broke in two,

Mum said
"listen girls and boys,
I've had enough,
there's too much noise."
"It isn't us", the dragons cried,
"I think it's coming from outside."

And as their things
flew round the cave,
Drop-it-all Dragon
got very brave.

He dived around  and caught a cup,

some plates fell down,

he scooped them up.

He saved a painting

with his wings,
his tail stretched out

and held more things.

The dragons all began to joke,
as not a single thing had broke!

The family laughed,
        their breath all hot.

"Drop-it-all Dragon,
you caught the lot!"

If you liked this book you will love this one:

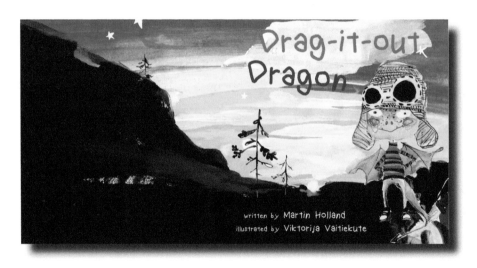

Drag-it-out Dragon, the first book in this series, where a cheeky young dragon leads his parents a merry dance whilst delaying his bedtime over and over again.

Available now from

www.dragitoutdragon.com